Beyond the Forest

Marie Silver

A novella

Marie Silver

ISBN - Paperback: 978-1-7383962-1-4
ISBN - Epub: 978-1-7383962-0-7

First Edition: May 2024

This book is dedicated to all of the late bloomers who are discovering and embracing their sexuality; no matter their age.

If you are 18+ and have an open curiosity.....Your sexual awakening starts on the next page.

Beyond the Forest

Marie Silver

Note from the Author:

This story includes themes of sexual intimacy, bdsm kink as well as strong sexual language. If any of that causes you discomfort we recommend you stop reading now. Should you choose to proceed with reading this novella, you are acknowledging and taking responsibility for choosing to do so.

Table of Contents

chapter One

My mouth goes dry as my pussy involuntarily clenches, sending a tingle of electricity past my belly button as it races to the tip of each nipple. I can feel them grow hard as they strain against my bra. It's been so long. Too long. I shift in my seat, needing to create some friction as I close my eyes and take in the booking notes.

I set my drink down on the coffee table as there's not much time before his arrival. I head over to the cabin to ensure the place is prepped and ready. I have the wine he chose, the aged scotch, and I turn down his bed. I recheck the booking details, not wanting to miss anything. It's important that I provide the best possible experience for each of my guests.

My breath catches as I notice that he paid for the upgraded package. My heart starts to race. My breathing picks up as I feel a warm flush spread across my body. I run one hand instinctively up my hip, the feel of my jeans rough on my palm.

My hand roams up my torso until I clutch my breast, squeezing it lightly. I groan as my hardened nipple sends shocks down my body.

I slowly run my hand up to my neck as I let my head fall back and enjoy the slow seduction of my own touch. I bite my lip as my thoughts begin to stir, exploring all the possibilities to come; I can't wait until he arrives. My mind runs through the list of services that he requested; what started as nerves turns to anticipation as I feel butterflies in the pit of my stomach. I'm nervous, I'm excited, and I know just how I will present them.

As time is ticking away, I jolt myself out of my daydream and spring into action. As I walk down the hallway I slide my hand into my pocket to fetch the key to access the closet. My skin is so alive and eager for his touch, I can't help but to think of his hands on me; with only a thin layer of fabric separating us.

I can feel how wet I am all over again at that thought. "*Common Renee, we aren't ready for him yet! Focus.*" I reluctantly pull the key from my pocket and unlock the door. I breathe in as I see the shiny blue trunk with gold hammered studs along the edges. I open it and excitedly reach for everything he asked for…the toys, the floggers, the restraints, the nipple clamps, and the glass butt plug.

Back to business. I grab the lube and the extra towels as I close the closet door with my bare foot to bring everything to the bedroom.

I set his room up by placing the tools on the wooden dresser. I turn to the bed and secure the straps of the restraints to each bed post. I place the lube and extra towels on the nightstands.

I then go to the living room and place the giant wooden X cross in front of the window. The light plays off the shiny brass bolts holding the leather straps in place. They are just waiting to be fitted around someone's wrists, waist, and ankles.

The view is perfect. It's as if you are stepping outside surrounded by nothing but the woods, birds, and the animals. The wall of windows connects the indoors to the outdoors, as the landscape lighting creates a soft romantic atmosphere as the soft large snowflakes fall from the sky.

Now that everything is perfect for his arrival, I run back to the main house, to change…

chapter Two

Goosebumps break out across my smooth skin as I anticipate every sound, every order, every touch, and every feeling to come…my soft white skin goes cold as I shiver with excitement. I wonder what his voice will sound like as he barks his orders; but before all of that can begin, what words will he string together to seduce my mind? How will he awaken the submissive slut inside, encouraging her to let go of all thinking and be focused solely on him?

The excitement in the unknown has my panties feeling damp as my thoughts spiral with anticipation. How will his muscles ripple as he lifts and tosses me into positions just right for his use? Which tool or will it be a toy, will he choose first? What will his first command be? What room will he choose to undress me in? How many times will he have me cumming before him? How I love the unexpected anticipation and excitement of a new guest.

As I allow my mind to wander, I spritz my favourite perfume under each ear, along my neck and on both wrists. I lather lotion on both of my legs, starting by gliding my lotion filled palm over my ankles, my calves and up my thighs until my hands cup each butt cheek, ensuring not a piece of skin is missed.

As I stand naked in my bedroom allowing the lotion to dry, I place the diamond stud earrings in my ears and let my hair down. My long brown hair falls as it covers my shoulders down to my bare lower back. I peruse the many outfits in the closet, letting the lace and silk dance along my finger tips. I really am grateful to own such beautiful pieces.

Some I bought, most I was gifted over the years; all having their own experiences and memories to share. I find the piece I was looking for and take it down off the hanger. I hold it up in front of me so it rests against my chest as I admire my partially naked reflection in the oversized full length mirror.

"Stunning, you are absolutely stunning. Let's go play, Renee."

chapter Three

It's been a long few weeks and God knows I deserve a break. My bosses moved up the schedule without consulting me first. Again. *Always working for the man, with little respect or appreciation in return.* I mumble to myself as my hands grip the steering wheel.

I can feel it in my veins as my blood races, the lack of control continues to slip from my grasp no matter how many overtime hours I put in.

Every so often, a man needs to escape by treating himself to a moment in time where he controls everything. This deep primal need to control every detail of a situation for both of our ultimate pleasure. Not only a desire, but a pent up need that latches itself so deep inside, you feel restless and on edge until you release it.

From describing every movement and every touch, to guiding the thoughts of another. Leading the emotions and physical sensations my eager sub will experience, all by taking some much needed R&R time.

As I anticipate the planned scene, I can feel my jeans getting tighter. The once racing blood in my veins is finally slowing its pace as the buzzing in my head subsides. I can feel his need taking over in my thoughts as I drive closer and closer to the cabin.

I have to...No, I need to take control of an eager submissive and coax out her inner slut like a blossoming flower. Only then will I finally find a sense of peace.

As I watch her follow my guidance, upon hearing her moans and the way her body reacts to my touch...... It's like the waves crashing into the shoreline, instantly relaxing and I feel myself becoming complete again.

I see the cabins come into view as I turn onto the lane. As I approach I feel the stress slip away and my balls tighten. *Renee has been very accommodating taking my last minute request. Maybe I will take it slow, feel it out before we begin.* I ponder as I sit parked in front of my assigned cabin.

I take a deep breath in. It's time I put my need to control a willing submissive in action.

chapter Four

"Welcome to my world, Sir." I smile as I watch him step through the door into the cabin, stopping mid step. watching as his eyes roam over every inch of me as I sit here in my favourite chair staring into his eyes.

My legs crossed where my ankles meet, my calf accentuated from the black stilettos covering my feet. His eyes move up my thighs and pause while his breath hitches as he takes in the lacey edges of the stocking, with a hint of a garter strap showing under the edge of my silk kimono.

"Hello Renee, you're looking lovely. Are you ready to play, once i get settled here?"

His deep, strong voice sends shivers through me causing my skin to break out with goosebumps as my pussy clenches and clit tingles. I can feel my nipples start to harden.

All of this just from his voice? Shiiiiiiit.

"You're biting your lip Renee. Is there something on your mind?"

As he speaks, I watch his cocky smile grow with each word as he holds my eye contact. His confidence and strength radiating from every inch of his tall husky frame. It's at this moment I sense I may have more than I bargained for with this one.

chapter **Five**

My mind is cluttered with all sorts of things, Sir. First of which is fetching you your drink. As I do, why don't you get yourself all settled?"

"There are fresh towels in the bathroom and the shower runs hot. Once you are settled, it will be your job to declutter this busy brain of mine."

I smile as I stand up and point towards the bedroom. I enjoy having the control in the beginning, giving direction and watching as the strong alpha follows it. It is the ones who do so without questioning that unknowingly turn me on the most.

I take in his wide shoulders, his long strong arms, licking my lips as I watch his ass, filling out those jeans perfectly as he walks away. I can tell he's a hard working man, most likely, underappreciated for all he does. I feel myself biting my lip again as I pour his bourbon straight up, thinking to myself I'll be sure to show him plenty of appreciation……

chapter Six

I hear the water turn off as I set his drink down on the dresser in his bedroom. As he opens the door from the ensuite, I slip out, back to the kitchen to finish pouring myself a glass of bourbon.

As I sip I can feel the warmth from the whisky flush my skin, creeping across my chest as it burns down my throat. The record stops playing, so I walk to the unit, glass in hand, as I peruse which record I will select instead. That's when I sense him enter the room and I instantly set my glass down.

"Turn around Renee and untie that robe. Let it fall slowly off your shoulders as you step towards me."

I see he's sitting down on the oversized leather recliner, which usually has people shrinking in size yet he's filling the entire chair. He knows how to command a room as I immediately follow his direction.

"Yes sir" I say as my hands untie the sash from the robe I've been wearing. As I take steps forward, I hear the click of my heels over the soft jazz as it plays in the background. I slide my hands up my lace covered torso, feeling my skin sizzle under my touch. The anticipation creates a buzz in my head and goosebumps appear along my skin. I feel the silk slide off my shoulders as my palms graze my breasts. The room grows hotter the closer I step to him. His intense stare doesn't hide his arousal. I caught that hitch in his breath the moment my robe slipped down to the floor.

"Sit on my lap, straddling me, as you look straight into my eyes."

"Yes sir"

I can feel his shaft already hard, constrained in his jeans as I sit down. My legs spread over his thighs as he takes each ankle to place the soles of my feet flat against the arm rests of the chair. My knees up and spread wide, hugging the sides of his torso. I can smell my sex wafting between us as I stare into his eyes.

With my hands on each arm rest to maintain my balance I await instruction. My mind is racing as I anticipate his next move. I am so glad I have the pre-booking to take care of establishing the rules, outlining in detail what's allowed and what's not for each of us, along with clear expectations for punishment.

"Renee, do you remember your safe word?"

"Yes Sir"

"What is it"

"Red"

"Good girl. I'm feeling quite frustrated tonight, so keep that word close should you need to use it." He states in his deep booming voice, his eyes never leaving mine. So intense. So full of desire.

"Yes Sir." I whisper back; wanting to shrink under his intense stare.

I see him pick up his drink, my gaze breaks as he takes a sip. He sets it down as I hear "tsk tsk". It's quickly followed by the feeling of the other hand as it comes down strong on my thigh. **SMACK.** I jump at the surprise of it but I don't move far as his fingers grip down on my thighs holding me in place. *"Don't look away Renee. Watch the pleasure in my eyes as I play with you."*

He takes his other hand and allows his fingers to graze up my torso, across the outside of my breast to the strap holding up my 38D's in place. As he slips each strap off my shoulders, he kisses my neck, leading me to tilt my head and give him more area to explore.

I feel his hot wet tongue flick its way across my neck where he stops to nibble my ear. I didn't notice his other hand has since left my thigh and just as he bites my ear lightly, I feel my left nipple flinch in pain. His strong thumb and forefinger twisting, pinching and pulling my nipple until my breast pops out its cup. He continues the same on my right side, this time he bites my collarbone in sync with his pinching and pulling of my right nipple until it, too, is free from its cup.

My breathing has picked up, I moan under his touch and as I try to wiggle on his lap I feel his warm breath just under my right ear as he says

"Stay still Renee. Don't move."

"Yes Sir." I say as I feel the cool air on my bare hard nipples. I can feel my pussy pulsing with desire, the wet spot growing with need. His hands hold both of my breasts, as he squeezes them and runs his thumb across the tip of the hardened nipples. I shudder under his touch, just as he speaks.

" I'm going to fuck you, just when you think you can't take it any more. Just when you think you can't cum anymore, It's then I will fill your tight wet needy pussy with my cock."

He bends me backward as he devours each breast with his mouth. His tongue flicking and toying each nipple as his hands press into my back to add more pressure as if he needs every inch of me in his mouth.

I moan as I feel him stand up, lifting me in the air as he carries us to the window overlooking the backyard and sets me down. *"Get naked. Leave the heels and thigh highs on."*

He guides me back onto the X cross. “Stay still Renee”. I feel the leather cuffs being placed on each wrist and watch as his lips glide down my naked body as he bends down to attach each ankle in their cuffs.

As I am held in place, naked and spread for him, in my most vulnerable state, he whispers in my ear. *“Renee, you are fucking stunning on display like this.”*

“Touch me sir, please” I whisper.

“Aww, Renee. You needy little cumslut, so eager.” as he walks around looking at the tools I placed out as directed, earlier in the day.

“I’m going to have you cum 3 times for me. You will ask permission to cum, every time, understand?”

“Yes Sir”

I watch Sir as his hands run across the tools, slowing as they feel the cool metal under his finger tips. I can just see the glass dildo and a pair of nipple clamps next to his palm.

“Mmmmmm, yes” I murmured.

“Oh Renee, do you like these toys?”

“Yes Sir”

"Is your eager pussy wanting to be filled?"

"Yes Sir. Please Sir." I groan.

He chuckles to himself as he hides his choice of tool behind his back. My skin feels ablaze under his stare, watching him watching me as he approaches. My nipples are so hard and I can feel my pussy dripping down my thigh in eager anticipation the closer he gets.

Without breaking eye contact, Sir takes the left breast into his palm as his thumb rubs over my hardened nipple, making me moan in pleasure with each touch. He breaks eye contact as my moan urges his mouth to take over where his thumb left off. I feel his teeth bite down as he flicks the tip of the nipple with his tongue, my groan and moan filling the room.

He pulls back smiling at me as he uses his left hand to pull my nipple as he uses the right to open the clasp and set it in place. The pink bud squeezed by the clamp as he proceeds to repeat on the right breast.

He drops his left hand down my torso as he reaches down toward my pussy, his finger just gliding over the hood of my clit.

"Ohhhhh fuuuuuuuuck" I groan as I wiggle my arms and legs pulling at the cuffs needing more. The clinking and clatter of the cuffs against the wooden X fill the room. I hear his deep chuckle as he clamps the right nipple while slipping two fingers into my wet eager pussy.

"Oh God…….Mmmmmmm yes sir " I moan as I feel the pinch of the clamps on my nipples as he jiggles the chain connecting them, as he thrusts his fingers in and out of my pussy repeatedly.

"Good Girl. I think someone is enjoying themselves." He takes his fingers from my pussy and slips them into my mouth.

I open my mouth as I feel his fingers brush across my lips, tasting my sweet juices on them. I suck on his fingers as I stare into his eyes, my tongue licking up and down as a moan escapes me.

"Mmmmm, I taste so good" I whisper.

His fingers continue to move rapidly in and out as his thumb, now rubbing my hardened clit. He kisses me hard. Our tongues battle each other, back and forth as we take in the taste of each other and my sweet salty juices perfume the air between us

"Cum for me Renee. Now." he demands as he breaks our passionate kiss.

I feel the orgasm building as he changes the motion of his fingers. They're now pressing forward on my walls toward my pelvis, in a come hither motion. Making the intensity inside me build more and more. I feel my lower abdomen start to contract, my pussy walls clenching hard down on his fingers and just as I'm about to release. I remember..

"Can I cum sir?" I whisper

"Yes. Now Renee." He demands as he presses back against my pussy walls not allowing them to be pushed out as I orgasm.

"Mmmmmm ooooooooohhhhhh fuuuuuuuuuckkkkkk , thank you sir" I moan out as my voice raises octave levels as I cum. As I do, I feel the blood rush to my nipples as the clamps are pulled off at the perfect time.

I'm left shaking and sweaty, panting as the orgasms flow through me. As I enjoy the post orgasm peace, I feel a warm wet firm sensation on my highly sensitive clit. It's then I realise it's his tongue. He must have dropped to his knees just as I finished cumming, when my eyes were closed.

I feel his tongue lick across my pussy lips right up to my clit. He licks again and again every inch of my pussy, from the clit to my labia, and the inner walls as he thrusts his tongue in and out. Fucking me.

He sucks and licks, making my very sensitive clit harder. He thrusts the glass dildo into my pussy. "Oh fuuuuuck sir" I moan as I feel it filling and stretching me. He thrusts it in and out of my pussy again and again as his tongue flicks my clit. You can hear the cuffs banging against their holder, as I wiggle and squirm in pleasure.

It's my favourite dildo, it has little bumps along the shaft that teases the inner walls every time it moves.

Making every cell wake up and take notice. My moans are building, I can't believe how loud I am being, how loud HE's making me be.

My brain has barely caught up to what he's doing to my body when I scream *"Can I come again Sir. Please. Now?"*

"Yes you may, my good slut." His demand is muffled as his mouth barely lifts up while he continues to thrust the dildo into my pussy as his tongue applies pressure on my clit.

He keeps me filled even as I feel my pussy walls pushing back against that dildo, as I release he holds his motions. I moan so loud, it's a high pitched whale between pants of breath.

"Mmmm good girl, that's two." He whispers as he stands. His beard glistens with moisture.

He unlatches each of my arms and ankles from the cuffs, as I slump down against him he carries me to the hammock. It hangs between two trees just off from the garden that borders the hot tub and forest beyond.

"Renee, lie face down ass up, across the width of this hammock. Your ass towards me, I want you facing the forest."

"Yes Sir" I reply as I stretch out the hammock and lay across it.

It takes a second to get placed correctly, once I do, I feel the tension of the ropes and knots against my skin. My nipples and breasts are poking through. It's one of those old school hammocks, the roped ones like fishnet stockings. The rope digs into my flesh as I press my chest down, doing my best to arch by keeping my ass up in the air.

"Let's see how good your throat skills are." He unzips his pants as he walks around the hammock, I watch as he comes towards me with his hand in his pants as he takes out his hard, throbbing cock. I can see the pre-cum that's been building, making me lick my lips so eagerly wanting a taste.

"You'll take all of me. No teeth. Worship this cock like the good cumslut you are" he commands as he looks down at me. I can see his desire burning in his eyes.

I open my mouth as I look up at him, watching as he places the tip of his cock in my mouth after a few taps on my face. My lips close around his tip, my tongue quickly slipping underneath to his most sensitive spot, just below the ridge.

I suck and lick as I feel him pressing more and more of his cock into my mouth. I grab his shaft with one hand as I hold myself up with the other, sucking and moaning as I worship it. His hands are in my hair, pulling it back out of my face into a ponytail.

He uses it to swing me on the hammock as he fucks my throat, back and forth, every time making me take more of him until my nose hits his base.

"Goooooooood girrrrrl" he growls.

I gag as I swallow his cock, the tip pressing against the back of my throat. My eyes water as I drool. Just when I think I need to breathe, he swings me away as he pulls his cock from my lips. *"Such a good cumslut you are."*

He grunts at me as he watches the drool from my lips fall down onto his cock, mixing with his pre-cum. He lifts his cock in the air as he brings my nose and mouth against his balls encouraging me to suck them. I do so eagerly, as I suck one ball then the other into my mouth massaging them with my tongue. The more he groans, the more I massage wanting to hear him groan again and again.

He pulls back and walks around behind me. He grabs the hammock edge on either side of my knees, pinning my legs up in the air spreading them as best he can.

"Ready to cum again for me Renee?" He whispers behind me, just as I go to respond I gasp.

The blood rushing to my head, the sensations of being stretched and filled so quickly and unexpectedly has my mind turn off.

I can only focus on the contact and pleasure of his body claiming mine. I hear him gasp as he slips his cock between my lips.

"Fuuuuck Renee, so tight." He groans as his thrusts grow faster. He uses the swing of the hammock to his advantage so it does not take long before we both cry out in pleasure as he fills me with his hot seed. It's then I hear *"Cum now Renee."*

As he flicks and rubs my clit, my ass in the air, it doesn't take but a minute as I explode from my third orgasm. I'm lost in the post cumming bliss as I feel him slide out of me. He picks me up from the hammock and carries me to his bed.

As he lays me down to rest, I hear him whisper as he leans down to my ear

"Good girl. Sleep well Renee."

chapter Seven

As I lay next to Renee, I feel strong and in control of myself again. I watch her sleep as I admire how I put that subtle smirk on her lips.

I'm so grateful for her willingness to explore her sensuality with me. To have someone, a stranger to boot, put total trust in my hands means more than she'll ever truly understand. I feel validated, larger than life as I lay here like a king. I made it safe for her to let go and I am honoured she let me.

I can't wipe the smile off my face as I turn to hold her against my chest. I always love this moment, when my submissive now cumdrunk, sleeps peacefully next me. How can a man not feel damn proud?

As I drift to sleep, my dreams are filled with visions of the coming morning's scenes. I chuckle lightly to myself as I whisper, *"Sleep well my little goddess, for you have no idea when I'll be slipping back inside you. Your ass needs attention too."*

The End

about the Author

Marie Silver is a single woman on her sexual awakening, after spending her lifetime following the rules and expectations set out by her faith, her church, and her family.

The fear of judgement and shame so great it kept her hiding the sensual side of her personality. Which is not easy for a Sagittarius.

After a life altering injury left her on forced medical leave; she has rediscovered her passion for writing. Her soul driven purpose is to create a series of mini stories that will keep your toes curling and temperatures rising with every word.

Let the words seduce your mind, leave the world behind, and just focus on the sensations you can create as you play.

Embrace your sexual energy whether with another consenting adult or for some much needed solo play. Crease those steamy pages and enjoy yourself.

Let Marie know how much you enjoyed this story by leaving her a 5 star review.

Coming **Soon**

In 2024, the next Novella from Marie Silver.
Sneak peak on the next page.

Above the **Clouds**

Flight 591 departing Toronto, Ontario has been delayed. Just long enough so I am no longer the last one arriving at the gate. This 'vacation' coming at the most inconvenient time.

My heart is racing as I sit here trying to catch my breath without my panting becoming noticeable. I cut the timing close. I didn't anticipate the traffic or the long line up thru security, but somehow I made it. Just breathe, in thru the nose, out thru the mouth. I focus my breathing as I get grounded before the flight. The only way to calm my pre-flight anxiety.

"Excuse me Miss, you dropped this."

I look up to see the most beautiful hazel eyes, looking right back at me. In his hand, is my phone. It must of slipped from my lap while I was taking a moment for myself.

"Oh. Thank you. That would have made for a very boring flight if I lost it." I reply as I take my phone from his hand.

I notice his smirk as he turns and walks away, just as the boarding call booms through the overhead speakers.

I find my seat and barely glance at the person sitting next to me. I'm tired, stressed out and trying to keep my shit together as I get settled. *You'd think with all the flying I do, this chest tightening, breathe stealing, sweat inducing anxiety would be a thing of the past.*

Closing my eyes again, I continue with my breathing exercises as I lean my head back against the seat. It's not long after I hear a slight chuckle beside me. I notice his long legs first, hunched up in the tight space. His woodsy scent drifting over filling my lungs as I breathe it in.

My ear tingles as a whisper of breath breezes across my skin, followed by the low, deep voice of the passenger sitting next to me.

"Seems you need a distraction, Miss."

"What makes you think, I need....." I stop speaking as I turn to face those stunning hazel eyes from earlier.

To be continued.

www.ingramcontent.com/pod-product-compliance
Lightning Source LLC
LaVergne TN
LVHW052107160826
845678LV00015B/3412

* 9 7 8 1 7 3 8 3 9 6 2 1 4 *